J. B. Crocker

My physician, Mind - Metaphysics in a Nutshell

a concise treatise on mental and spiritual dynamics - their application as a

therapeutic agent, in the cure of all diseases, whether in acute or chronic

form

J. B. Crocker

My physician, Mind - Metaphysics in a Nutshell
a concise treatise on mental and spiritual dynamics - their application as a
therapeutic agent, in the cure of all diseases, whether in acute or chronic form

ISBN/EAN: 9783337390167

Printed in Europe, USA, Canada, Australia, Japan

Cover: Foto ©Andreas Hilbeck / pixelio.de

More available books at **www.hansebooks.com**

My Physician, Mind.

Metaphysics in a Nutshell.

A CONCISE TREATISE ON

Mental and Spiritual Dynamics.

Their Application as a Therapeutic Agent, in the Cure of *all Diseases*, whether in *Acute* or *Chronic* Form.

IN SCOPE,

It covers the entire domain of Man's relations to *God*, the *Neighbor*, and to the *Universe* of *Things*.

Mind is a universal prophylactic; it renders both body and soul impervious to all moral or physical perturbations.

TOPEKA, KANSAS:
Geo. W. Crane & Co., Printers and Binders.
1886.

PREFACE.

MUCH has been said and written of late on the subject of Metaphysical Pathology and Therapeutics. Of necessity, each author has mapped out his own cluster of conceptions, amplified his premises, and intensified his fundamental idea; and, in some instances, its power in healing has been demonstrated.

No uniform Theory or Practice has, as yet, been established, save the proposition of a general denial of the existence of matter on the one side, and the affirmation that "All is Mind," on the other. Much of the thought-matter heretofore published has had its origin in the personal experience of the writer, rather, than in an adaptation to, and an outcome from, the *fitness* of *things*, made manifest in universal nature.

The public mind is ready to welcome any new movement having for its end the alleviation of human suffering, and which would pave the way for the expression of higher and purer conditions of life.

Health and disease are fundamental questions, interwoven with the dearest interests of all mankind, in their individual, as well as, their collective capacity.

The present writer is fully conscious that much good has already resulted from the agitation of thought in this direction. But a vast amount of missionary work remains to be done; for the fields are white unto harvest, and the *real*—the genuine, *unselfish workers*—are few.

It may seem merely analogous and prophetic to state, that the day is not far distant when a wave of divine harmony will reach this planet, and the *rule of righteousness be applied to the affairs of every-day life*. Then all-sided perfection in individual character will be attained. Sin and sickness will be things of the past, and all public institutions will be the highest expressions of Divine Love and Wisdom. "My Physician, Mind," is sent forth to aid its coming.

> Aid its dawning, tongue and pen;
> Aid it, hopes of honest men.
> Aid it, paper—aid it, type;
> Aid it, for the hour is ripe.
> And our earnest must not slacken into play;
> Men of thought and men of action, clear the way.

TABLE OF CONTENTS.

CHAPTER I.

BASIC PRINCIPLES.

God, the Universe, Man.

Soul and Spirit.

Spirit and Mind.

Mind and Body.

Body and Environment.

These all exist as *Relative Opposites* and *Mutual Dependents*. They are merely the antithetical repetitions of the *higher* in the *lower*, and *vice versa*, reciprocally.

ONTOLOGICAL.

STATEMENT OF BEING.

BEING is both passive and active. Its passive side corresponds to the absolute and infinite. It is the boundless ocean of unconscious thought—the limitless sea without a shore. Its active side is the *relative*, the *finite*, which enters into, or rather, *represents*, the *infinite*, being its expression. *Being* is the repository of all forces and their formative processes.

Being is self-extant—lies back of and beyond all prime elements and principles,

ideas and their illustrations. It is an unbroken unit, unlimited by time, space, sense
or soul.

All forms and forces *derive* their *existence*.
They are but the manifestations of that *Infinite Fountain* of principles, interior, anterior
and posterior to all motion, life and sensation,
throughout all domains of thought.

Being, or God, the Absolute and All-em-
bracing, as an *Infinite Unit*, remains eternally
in *statu quo*, *without* beginning, end or change.
All that was, is. To the whole nothing can
be added—nothing taken from—since it
takes all the parts to constitute the whole.

God, the *I Am*, is more than Principle and
Personation; more than Unity and Variety;
more than the Universal and Particular;
more than *Life*, *Truth* and *Love*, *Substance*
and *Intelligence;* for these exist in endless
modifications, and the eternal wisdom which
combines all is *less* than "*God*, blessed forevermore."

God cannot be comprehended, for the reason that that which is comprehended is *less*
than the comprehendor. It would be com-
pressing the whole within the limits of a part.
A proper thought and understanding thereto
is possible, but this knowledge can only be

attained through the Soul's connection with God.

The *procedure* or manifestation of *force*, *vis*, *life*, or the subtle, creative essence, does not emanate from one single power alone. The Infinite Father involves the Infinite Mother as its relative opposite and mutual dependent. The *Brotherhood* of the race has a diviner complement, a "better half," in the *Sisterhood* of the race. As it is written, (Gen. I, 26): "And God said, Let us make man in our image, after our likeness; and let them have dominion over the fish of the sea, and over the fowl of the air, and over the cattle, and over all the earth, and over every creeping thing that creepeth upon the earth."

The Infinite and Finite, male and female, are the "*us*," the inseparable two, in one. Unity is complemented in the infinite variety, displayed in contrasted elements, uni-variety, two in one. The omnipresent and everlasting change has *its* relative opposite and mutual dependent in the *inexpugnability* of *prime elements*. In every change there is always a persistent remainder. The Creator and the creature are but reflections of each other—*two in one*.

There is no substance but *that* made manifest *through form*. All objective forms are
but illustrations of interior forces, (Mental
and Spiritual Dynamics,) thoughts and intellectual perceptions on the one side, and intuitional, emotional energies on the other
side. The former represents the male element; the latter the female. These acting
and reacting upon one another, bring Life
and Immortality to light.

In the beginning God created the heaven
and the earth. "And God said, Let there
be light, and there was light." Light was
the result of the Word (thought, impulse).

"In the beginning was the Word, and the
Word was with God, and the Word was
God. The same was in the beginning with
God. All things were made by Him; and
without Him was not anything made· that
was made."

The word "beginning" has no value when
exclusively applied to time, for the universal
symbol of duration is an unbroken circle,
without beginning or ending.

Time is only the comparative degrees of
motion over space. Day and night, spring-
time and harvest, summer and winter, are
merely *results* from the diurnal and annual

revolutions of the earth. The common time piece is constructed upon the same principle, the different motions being indicated upon the circle of the dial. *Beginning* must have reference to the Word, thought or intention, the formative force from which the earth and its atmosphere resulted, and these could have had but a *relative* beginning, since they are reflections of God and the Word—*two in one.*

The form and substance constituting the earth and heaven never had a beginning as prime elements. They are reflections of God's thought, but, through new combinations, are forevermore producing new expressions; and these expressions are the outcomes of *Mental and Spiritual Dynamics.*

And God said: "Let us make man in our image, after our likeness." Man is the result of a *dual force*, and his constitutional make-up is—

Male and Female,
Positive and Negative,
Finite and Infinite,
Absolute and Relative,
Form and Substance.

These are all expressed in infinite degrees

of variation—no two expressions ever being the same.

Man is the *perfect image* and *exact likeness* of *God.* The Soul of Man forms a complete circle—is a *perfect entity.* The life of the Soul is immortal, and this immortality has reference alike to past, present and future— is related to God in the ratio of the atom to the whole. The innermost of the circle or sphere of the soul represents the female principle; the outer, the male principle— two in one. The former is the more spiritual; the latter more intellectual.

The soul does not dwell *within* the *body,* any more than God dwells *within* the *soul,* or the painter within the picture. The soul is the absolute and infinite principle—God's perfect idea.

The life of the soul is broken into two halves, or, rather, one-half is *eclipsed* or shaded, like evening chasing the morning, darkness the light. These two distinctive features of consciousness are relative opposites and mutual dependents, complementary to each other. The Absolute side is the fountain source of all aspiration, and forms the background of the picture of all spiritual expressions and human endeavors; it constitutes the *better self*, toward which man is forever reaching, and, through which, he discovers Deity, develops individual reason and intuition, and recognizes the beautiful law of interdependence and divine harmony.

Spirit, in contradistinction to *Soul*, refers to that side forming the connection between the *celestial* and the *terrestrial;* it is represented in the organic structure as the neck which connects the head with the trunk. It is the dynamic force which forms all organs and repairs all injuries. The spiritual consciousness is broken by three elements, viz., by time, space, and the senses, and becomes subject in its visible expression to the action of the outer laws of the universe.

The experiences entered upon by the soul, through the spirit, in connection with the body, are infinite in their variety; and, are carried forward uninterruptedly from one point of culmination to another; therefore, *each experience* makes its record *upon the being of the soul*, as the rings within the tree denote the years of its growth.

The soul's descent, through the spirit into limitations, is symbolized in Genesis, third

chapter. The "Eden" condition, or Para-
dise, represents man previous to his coming
in contact with the corporeal principle (matter, if you please); for, his *descent* was a
direct spiritual impulsion, an *aggregation* of
prepared atoms, and *not* through generation;
for, marriage, as yet, had not been instituted.

Man, the human, was a spiritual creation,
and did not come to the earth alone; but,
like the atoms, the stars, the flowers, came
in groups; consequently, an orderly and or-
ganized condition of life is the natural
state of man; hence, the family, society,
community, etc. The spiritual ties being
stronger and more enduring than the ties of
consanguinity, accounts for the discord existing among blood relations; such are not of
the same group, or of the same spiritual
household.

All forms in objective life result from the
attrition and *coalescence* of *relatively opposing
forces,* which are harmonious, or otherwise,
in the exact ratio of parallelism entering into
such association or marriage of relatively opposing forces. This fact is basic and founda-
tional. It forms the key of harmony in the
constitution and construction of all things;
it is exemplified in the atomic structure of

worlds and systems of worlds; and applies, with equal force, to man and all man-made institutions.

CHAPTER II.

MENTAL and Spiritual Dynamics involve those forces which are expressed in the domain of the senses; they are amenable to human power externally applied, on the one side, and that vast, subtle, invisible force, *not amenable* to human power externally applied, on the other side. Together, they constitute all organs, being the organizer; all functions, with their operating and repairing forces; all the faculties and the inspiration that infills them. They exist as male and female—are relative opposites and mutual dependents; and, through their attrition and coalescence, human life is sustained and the species perpetuated.

Man is surrounded by silent forces, which play upon his senses in a vague and undefined manner. He breathes them in the atmosphere; absorbs them through contact;

[16]

assimilates them in the processes of nutrition; discovers them by thought, idea, and perception in form and substance; catches their vibrations and tones of harmony through the ear; sees their beauties through the eye; knows and communes with them through the *affection* and *wisdom faculties*, the outermost laws of which, in a very limited sense, only, have been discovered and applied to ultimate use; while the innermost laws of which, have, as yet, not been dreamed of by any mind on earth.

Remember, that for every ultimate physical atom there is a correlative, spiritual force; for every ultimate physical result, there is a correlative spiritual cause; for every manifestation of matter defined by the intellect, there is a *spiritual cause not defined* by the intellect—not yet reached by science.

Mind, alone, is positive. Spirit, alone, is elemental, indestructible, primal. That which is combined can be disintegrated; that which is an aggregation of atoms can be changed and its form destroyed.

But *Soul* is the one sole primate—never combines, is indestructible, changes not, passes not away; is ancient as God, coeval with His spirit, born of His breath, living in

His life; does not have its birth on earth; is not the result of physical organism; does not proceed from combinations of matter, favorable to the production of essences, called mind.

Man, the epitome of material creation, is also the expression on earth of a spiritual creation. Where material science pauses, spiritual science begins with its wonderful wealth, its knowledge of all past and future things — a revelation which transcends the senses and brings to human consciousness the truth that there is no lost link in the chain of being. *Thought never perishes*, but abides forever; it builds the temples of the future, and paves the way for more exalted states of existence, of which we have, to-day, no more knowledge than has the material scientist of the *primal atom* of matter which, as yet, has not been found.

Spiritual dynamics has given proof of its potency in the broad illustrations of universal worlds, and throughout the separate kingdoms each may contain — in the pulling down of old forms, and their reconstruction into the more beautiful new. It has verified its wonder workings, in the domain of the human senses, in *apparently suspending* the

forces of cohesion and attraction, by causing
bodies of equal density to pass silently and
rapidly through one another; as in *levitation*,
overcoming the law of gravitation; Jesus
walking upon the sea; persons floating
through the air; ponderous bodies moving
without any visible contact; also, as in *ma-
terialization*, the instantaneous production of
beautiful, fragrant flowers, luscious fruits,
and the like; converting water into wine;
feeding five thousand hungry people with
five loaves and two small fishes, and gather-
ing up twelve baskets that remained; taking
from *fire* its power to consume the human
organism, while handling red hot coals; pass-
ing through the fiery furnace; in raising the
apparently dead; in healing the sick; taking
up venomous reptiles; in accordance with the
Master's promise, "If ye drink any deadly
thing, it shall not hurt you." It has been
displayed in the Fine Arts, tracing beautiful
fruits and flowers and familiar forms in the
mundane and super-mundane spheres; truth-
fully transferring the grand old mountains
and the gorgeous canons of Colorado upon
canvas, through the organism of a blind-
folded artist. It is the *force*, which in the
domain of mind, floods *human consciousness*

with sublime inspirations, making brilliant orators from untutored maidens, whose beauty and pathos have astonished the world; whose clear logic has confounded the skeptic with argument so complete that there remained no grounds for disputation; through it new ideas have been evolved, new thoughts of life, and what life portends; unfolding the purposes of being — its laws, and their application in uplifting processes of human progress; it has rolled back the stone from the Sepulcher, proving continuous life beyond the grave, opening up the beauties of inter-communion between the two worlds; it has brought to the home and hearth-stone of almost every family the intelligent presence of the long-mourned loved ones; it has broken down the barriers of superstitious fear; delivered from the thralldom of the senses, changing the grim monster, Death, into the white-winged messenger of immortal life and celestial glory.

This world presents the extremes of *poverty* and *riches, beauty* and *deformity, virtue* and *vice.* Human life is an endless combination of these extremes, which the Intellect is endeavoring to explain, Religion to reconcile, and Philosophy to harmonize.

These extremes are the natural results which must oûtflow from incomplete and imperfect comminglings of elements in the realm of thoughts, ideas and things; and *not* from the prime elements themselves. These are all-wise, beneficent and harmonious— God's perfect idea. The natural condition of man is an orderly, *not* a disorderly condition—a healthy, not a diseased one; and it is just as easy to organize for health as for sickness; for success, as for failure; for virtue, as for vice.

Through man's associations, combinations and organizations, the *dual forces* of his being find *expression*. His dependencies and compensations are limited and qualified by his associations. Any unsatisfied need through dependence not fully and adequately responded to, through compensation, is *prima facie* evidence that the sufferer is *ignorant* of the *law of association*, or, else, that the *law of association is incomplete in itself*. The prime elements in the vast association of universal nature, on the one side, and man-made institutions on the other, constitute the sum total of man's dependencies and compensations.

These dual principles which are discoverable in all domains of conscious thought are, in their distinctive contrasts, complementary, as parts to a whole. They make up the two halves which enter into man's being and the make-up of humanity; and, when they flow together harmoniously, as relative opposites and mutual dependents in man's institutions, as well as in the individual life, the acme of civilization will have been reached; and *poverty, pain, injustice, war and disease* will have been *outgrown*. These fearful calamities, now resting like a pall upon humanity, are only *danger signals*, held out to warn them against violated and abused relations — *tender appeals* to the "prodigal to arise and *go to his father*," rather than having any basis in truth.

The *scale or standard of compatibility between relative opposites and mutual dependents*, both in their simple and complex forms, may be rendered as simple and self-evident as the degrees of latitude which mark the various zones upon the planet, or as those of the thermometer, which indicate the relative degrees of heat. It may be applied, alike, to individuals, communities and nations, as well as to the universe of things; it is the standard for all elements combining for organization; it is a *universal criterion* and *system of equations*—the measure of all value and force.

The arm of all power and momentum being in association, combination and organization, the work before us is simple and self-evident, to wit: *The application of the law of relative opposites in sexology, parentage, population and ownership,* making it impossible for any one to be sick, deformed, insane or vicious, and forming a *prevention to divorce, adultery, and the begetting of imbecile children;* the application of this law to an *Integral System of Education,* in which proper facilities shall be afforded for the culture of the entire being; healthy action of all bodily organs; the development of vigorous intellectual powers; the evolution of intuitive and spiritual forces.

To apply the law of relative opposites in a comprehensive and all-sided system of scientific co-operation, in which *Capital and Labor* shall be divinely married, would advance the highest civilization, the natural outcome of which would flood the world with wealth, making it *impossible for any to be poor or uncultured.*

CHAPTER III.

SEXOLOGY, Parentage and Population do not result from one arbitrary power alone; they are the commingling of the complementals of *life, love, truth, substance* and *intelligence*. This truth is universal in its scope and application. Marriage covers the whole domain of life; it is evident in the mineral, vegetable and animal kingdoms. In *man*, it is the call and answer of his better self found in woman, bone of his bone, flesh of his flesh—the beauty of his life, and the completeness of his being. In *woman*, it is the *responsiveness to that call*—the spiritual to the material; the intuitional to the intellectual; the bearing, passive side, to the active, aggressive side; the joyous and loving assumption of the sacred and tremendous functions of maternity, with a sweet welcome and patient endurance of the vast responsi-

bilities involved in reproduction and the perpetuation of the race.

To understand sexology in its *entirety*,
constitutes the perfect law of life and the
perfection of human character, and *fulfilling
its conditions is the only intelligent obedience to
God*, the only *possible worship* of Him in the
beauty of holiness.

The science of marriage is the perfect
blending of the love-spirit in *use and beauty*
as relative opposites, when they are com-
patible, for a higher outcome. It is *Typeculture*, or the prefiguring of a higher type
of manhood in the ascending scale of being,
wherein the qualities of both parents are
united in a single expression—*a new birth,
a sublimer creation*.

Nothing exists outside the domain of
fecundatory movements in relative opposites; and they are intensified and widened,
exalted or lowered, in the *exact degree of
the parallelism in adaptation* to the constitution and make-up of the elements commingling. Correspondence and variation
are complements, both simple and complex;
as in the variation and continuity of silence
and sound, high and low pitch in the elements of music.

Harmony or discord is the result of the *association* in the *composition*, and not in the *elements* themselves; so, too, *all forms of evil, sin, sickness and death* are *not in prime elements. God never made them.* They originate *in* and *through combination*—are the offspring of marriage under the *regime* of immature thought, motive, perception and blind ignorance; they are, then, *circumstantial, not primal.*

Much has been said in regard to heredity and the transmission of qualities. The subject is daily widening and intensifying in interest; but, as yet, no basic ideas, no fundamental principles, have been discovered, or, if discovered, have not in any extensive manner been applied.

The transmission of qualities from one generation to another is not absolute, since nature never repeats herself—that is, she is infinite in her variety, there being no two expressions precisely alike. It is relatively true, all things being equal, that "like begets like." The leading qualities of both parents are generally represented in their offspring.

It is a common practice with the agriculturist to select situation, climate, soil, etc., with wise reference to the *nature and constit-*

uents of the seed sown, the tree planted; and,
in the process of growth, should one blossom be more perfect than the rest, he fructi-
fies the next best of its kind, or engrafts a
new stem upon the tree whose roots are
more thrifty and enduring than that which is
not indigenous; thereby he secures the very
best result as to quantity and quality; nothing short will satisfy his progressive mind.
So, too, the stock-raiser asserts the *divinity*
of his idea in selection through sexual blend-
ings; his sire and dam are chosen in refer-
enbe to his *object in the ultimate use* of the
offspring. If a draft horse be purposed,
weight, size, bone, muscle, in just proportion
to the requirement, are appealed to. He
has recourse to very different selections in
the production of a racer—*speed* is now the
dominal element sought for, with correspond-
ing proportions adapted to the use or service
to be performed, *functional activities* being
the only *formative force.*

Man is an active agent in the discovery
and application *to use* of all laws and forces.
He discovers these in their adaptation to the
conditions in the various zones of the earth;
their *indigenous* aspects are *indexes* to his
fertile mind, having in his thought their cor-

respondentials. The electric and magnetic fields of force are beginning to be recognized—the various tones and producing properties of sunlight are all more or less regarded to-day, and the discovery is not far distant when *mental and spiritual dynamics will have their place,* and be regarded the *divine art in reproduction.* It would indeed be very singular to contemplate an artist in whose mind there was not prefigured the image and idea he was about to transpose to the canvas. He would be a strange sculptor who did not behold in the rough block of marble his divine idea ere he applied the chisel. The architect has the entire plan of the edifice ere the foundation stone is laid; the inventor, his invention; the designer, his design.

What shall be said, then, in reference to *human typeculture?* Is there no royal grace prefigured upon the baby brow? No hyperion curls, no Jove-like front, no classic curves? Do not the stars laugh with joy when the mother endows her child with grace and beauty in her appeals to this *science of all sciences—human typeculture?* Does the father forget in the fiery throes of holy inspiration, and in the acme of his aspiration, does he fail to *plumb the line to fine proportions, classically to cut the precise adjustment* of corresponding parts? Beneath the emotional, underlying the senses—aye, even the consciousness, there exists an under-current of mental and spiritual forces not yet *fathomed*, not, as yet, understood.

The *body*, the *shell*, the *habiliments only*, are combined through marriage; under the *auspices* of the *spirit's suggestion* is the *body compounded*, the *germ selected*, through which the spirit fingers shall attune its human melo-dies through human experiences. It is the combination of elements, the *setting* for the precious jewel—the tabernacle for the Shekinah—in which the ever-burning and illuminating ray of spirit may act, be it for a century, be it only for an hour. Parentage furnishes the *body only*, the *fundamental premises, considered* from a *purely physical* standpoint. The incoming spirit which quickens, the emanation from soul's eter-nal sphere, hath no beginning—is *self-existent, self-affirming*.

In soul-life, the male and female forces were embodied in *one organism*, correspond-ing to the deep sleep "God caused to fall upon Adam" ere the "rib" was taken from his side — the passive side of being, the infinite, fathomless side, which is the relative opposite and mutual dependent of the *finite*, the *active* side.

The *spirit's sojourn* on the *planet* is *limited* by the *fulfillment* of its intention in the lessons gathered from outer consciousness through the experiences incumbent upon its embodied career. Some, only, come for a *moment*, just to *touch* again the earth's outer sphere, while others work a century or more. Moses made his exit at the age of one hundred and twenty years. "His eye was not dimmed, nor his force diminished." Environments, and their compatibility to perfect or imperfect expressions form a factor in the longevity of individual existence. If the circumstances be *too* intense for the degree of energy embodied, the spirit assumes another form, better adapted to fulfill its designs. It never returns from the field of battle without its laurels of victory, mind being *positive* to matter, spirit to sense, soul to circumstance.

The infinite variety of experiences which earth affords has to be entered upon by each and all; hence the pauper and peasant of one series of experience *may be* the autocrat in another, and *vice versa*, reciprocally. The

compensating forces in being are *absolutely*
and *relatively just.* No abuse of any of the
functions of life goes by *uncorrected by the
abuser himself.* When *this law is understood*,
no person *can afford* to act viciously or un-
wisely; it will *then* be discovered that *stealing*
is robbing one's self; and the hero of a thousand battles will learn that *murder* does not
kill.

"A sower went out to sow his seed; and
as he sowed, some fell by the wayside; and
it was trodden down, and the fowls of the
air devoured it. And some fell upon a rock;
and soon as it sprang up, it withered away,
because it lacked moisture. And some fell
among thorns, and the thorns sprang up
with it, and choked it. And others fell on
good ground, and sprang up, and bare fruit
an *hundredfold.*" In *typeculture, who* and
what the *wayside?* Who and what the *devouring fowls of the air*, but the *vile, secret
sin*, the *carrion raven of abortion?* Who
and what the *thorns*, but the mis-mated
—those out of parallelisms in wedlock?
Which the *rocky ground*, but the *extremes*,
the *incompatible conditions?* To raise the
standard of population in *morals*, in *intelligence* and in *environments*, is to *apply the law*

*of perfect physical and spiritual adaptation in
Sexology,* and the result will be the birth of
a royal brotherhood—a race of gods. "He
who hath ears to hear, let him hear."

CHAPTER IV.

Mental and Spiritual Dynamics
in reference to a
Universal System of Education,
in which
Mind and Body,
Intellect, Intuition and Emotion,
Abstract Ideas and their Practical Illustrations
are
Relative Opposites and Mutual Dependents.

EDUCATION and Mental and Spiritual Dynamics are *relative opposites* and *mutual dependents* in *themselves*, since *Education* is a *mental* and *spiritual process*—one mind acting on other minds—a *spiritual force acting on other spiritual forces.*

The distinction between *mind* and *spirit* is similar to that existing between *mind* and *body;* the body being the servant of the mind, in its functional operations is reached by the action of the faculties of the mind through the brain and nervous system. The mind, in turn, becomes the active agent in receiving and transmitting the motives, intention and designs of the rational-spiritual

3   [33]

from headquarters—the realm of Infinite Soul.

In the fitness of things, a *universal system of integral education* calls for a *universal language to express it.* The different languages of the earth did not arise, and do not exist, on account of any difference in form or sound as prime factors in speech. A *point,* a *line,* an *angle,* or any other form, is the same the world over. A tree is a tree, alike in Constantinople or Moscow. So the lungs and vocal organs are formed on the same universal principle. Even in the science of music, the *scale* is *uniform among all nations* and *races.*

Why, then, should the *human voice* give forth an uncertain sound? Why spend *time* and *force* to acquire an arbitrary and ambiguous dialect in order to make known to one another the significance of ideas, thoughts or objects, which in themselves are the *common property, known* and *understood* alike by all mankind? A universal language would, at least, relieve the mind from this onerous task, as well as to free language itself from its variety of contradictions and arbitrary dictum.

There *was* a period in the earth's history

when there was but one form of speech, but
one language. But, through the abuse of
this tremendous power proceeding from
unity, (for union is strength,) language was
broken into fragments by the Lord, ([Gen. 11,]
the man of the planet,) who came down and
scattered them abroad from thence upon the
face of all the earth (the grandest coloniza-
tion scheme ever inaugurated.) If this con-
fusion and dispersion was a penalty for the
trespass on the good order previously existing, if it were the *consequence* of an *error*, an
abuse, the *sooner* it is repented of, the *sooner*
will the lost arts of that primal age be re-
stored.

Education is continuous and life-long. It
consists in the knowledge of objects, their
relations and functional operations on the
one side, the active, spiritual principles, ideas
and intelligent purposes they were intended
to illustrate, on the other, as *relative opposites*
and *mutual dependents*. *Self-knowledge* on
the one side, *man* and *the universe of things*,
on the other, as *relative opposites* and *mutual
dependents*, — the *ideal* and *intellectual* on the
one side, the *experimental* and *practical* on
the other. The wise men of ancient Greece
considered an education the best possible

legacy they could transmit to posterity, and
had emblazoned in golden capitals upon their
magnificent temple at Delphos these immortal words, "Know Thyself." This is the
golden key which unlocks the inexhaustible
treasures of *Being* in its physical, mental and
spiritual aspects. It is the *revelator* of *God*
in *man*, the *neighbor*, and the *universe* of
things, together with all the rights and responsibility involved therein.

In an integral system of education, the
contrasted elements, *body* and *mind*, must
exist, and be sustained in *equatorial lines* of
compatibility as *relative opposites* and *mutual
dependents*. The same law maintains in the
associations of the intellect with the intuition
and emotions. The intellect corresponds to
the engine, the emotion to the steam; in
parallelism they are the *locomotive of mental
dynamics*. The intellect alone, like the engine without the steam, is lifeless, and the
intuition and emotion, without the modifying
force of the intellect, is void of expression.

Perfect as the present school system of
this country may be considered, it certainly
lacks those essential elements and facilities
for the ultimation and practical illustrations
of *abstract ideas*. It lacks the expressive

side, which can only be outwrought through the utilities of industrial science in *association with the elements necessary therefor*.   Education is not a system of *forced measures*, but a drawing out of that which is written, the *unfolding* of the *sacred scroll* upon which the *finger of God* has traced His own *absolute attributes*.

CHAPTER V.

MENTAL AND SPIRITUAL DYNAMICS
IN REFERENCE TO
A UNIVERSAL SYSTEM OF SCIENTIFIC COÖPERATION,
IN WHICH
CAPITAL AND LABOR,
PRODUCTION AND CONSUMPTION,
ARE
RELATIVE OPPOSITES AND MUTUAL DEPENDENTS.

HAVING *unbounded confidence* in the *progressive nature* and *infinite possibilities* of *man, mind,* also, in the wise ordination of all things in universal nature, we are fully assured, that, from the present conflicting elements the harmonies of a world-wide confederation *must emerge;* that, through the divine marriage of opposing forces, a new civilization must be born, which will embody in its constitution all *natural law,* which will express all *natural rights* and their *corresponding responsibilities,* growing out of all human relations; which will guarantee to all the *full opportunity* of *satisfying* their natural wants; thus harmonizing the *individual* and *collective interests* of humanity,

[38]

without reference to *race, nationality* or *sex*, uniting all into one *universal fraternal tie.*

To organize a universal system of scientific co-operation *challenges* the *best efforts* of the *foremost minds* upon the planet. In a comprehensive sense, organization appertains to the *discovery* of those *functional activities* which constitute the *formative force*—the begetting principle in universal nature. It is *absolute* and *despotic*—the *law of necessity*, the *rule of science.* In a popular sense, it alludes to any particular formula, rule, system of parliamentary usage, under which a variety of individualities flow together in a unitary or combined endeavor to ultimate the original designs of the organizers.

Father and Mother, the Creator in the stupendous and perfect mutuality of the universe, has written out the law of organization which covers the entire domain of man's relations. The lines of demarkation through all these relations are simple, self-evident, *universal in their scope and application;* at the same time, in their silent potency, *allwise* and *beneficent.* The student may turn his investigating eye to any one of earth's kingdoms, and he will discover this principle unfolded in infinite variety; or, should he in the piercing glances of astronomical research view the position of the mighty worlds moving in the vast, illimitable fields of ether, he will find there a perfect system of classification in group-life, cluster after cluster combining with each other and revolving round a common center. The beautiful *law of correspondence runs through all* with order and harmony; and, taking each part separately, or as a vast whole (as far as can be comprehended), it is alike marked with a *sacred wisdom* and *beauty* which time and space cannot encompass. The same principle that impelled the wonderful energies of the Divine Mind in the development of worlds throughout space—some a *million times larger than the earth*, and flying at a rapidity of over fifty thousand miles an hour, carrying with them in their orbits vast *retinues* of smaller worlds, all moving in *harmony* with *certainty* and *precision*, is alike applicable to the regulation and government of all human affairs in every relation of life.

No *system of co-operation*, or *form* of *government* can be *permanent* which does not admit of *universal application;* is *not scientific* and *natural* in its *origin; discovered,* and *not man-made.* It must proceed from the func-

tional necessity involved in the inherent nature of things, and which is decided by
scientific verities, and not by the voice of
the multitude.

The grand and all-pervading law of compensation, with its relative opposite, dependence, is the *fundamental law* of the *universe*,
and a system of mutual combination furnishes the only vehicle through which these
forces can operate in their natural and beneficent attrition; hence we see this law demonstrated not only in the form and
approximation of all things in objective
nature, from the innumerable systems of
planetary worlds through the separate kingdoms each may contain, to the *generic,
specific* and *individual expressions*, but also
in the highest operations of *supreme love* and
wisdom, through every gradation of thought
and feeling the human mind is susceptible to,
or *capable of*, even to the *faintest impulse* of
instinct in organic life.

As there cannot take place a single act but
what this law covers, and, as in the affairs of
life, there has never as yet been any order or
system of combination instituted *sufficiently
broad* to admit of the *full exemplification* of
this law in its *richness, beauty* and *beneficence*

in *man's relations*, these facts furnish ample
incentives to right effort in this direction, for
the law still acts, through unfavorable as
well as favorable conditions, giving *life* and
happiness, if *co-operated with*, or *poverty, pain,
disease* and *death*, if *infringed.*

That there is no defect in the universal
system of association, in point of form,
magnitude, position of each individual object, is evident from the harmonious result
observed throughout nature. The form
given to the planetary worlds, together with
their peculiar motions, is such as to secure,
not only, the most equal distribution of benefits flowing from the central source of light
and heat, as well as from all the sister orbs
in the group, but at the same time to give off
in return an equal amount, so that every
advantage is fully reciprocated. The same
principle operates in the existence and relations of every atom that has motion, life or
sensation.

No institution can endure which is not susceptible to universal application — *discovered,*
not *man-made* — inherent in man's constitution, and innate in the nature of things. It
must operate after the order of nature from
center to circumference, and *vice versa*, recip-

rocally—must be perfectly voluntary and
free. Its *cohesiveness* is derived from the fact
that all parts are held together by its life-
giving elements; the individual and collective
benefits it confers are so vital to success and
happiness, that to separate one'sself therefrom, would be an act of suicide.

Nature, and *Nature's God,* are the *only
capitalists.* The only wise God, an eternal
Father and Mother, are the only creators of
all prime elements of production. "In the
beginning God created the heaven and the
earth." "The earth," therefore, "is the
Lord's, and the fullness thereof." The Creator
has made ample provision for the functional
operation of consumption in man, which he
has himself imposed as an *arbitrary necessity*
to physical life. When He ordinated the in-
carnation of man, the earth and all that it
contained was entrusted to man as *man,* for
his benefit and wise use. In the infancy of
the race, the spontaneous productions of the
earth and sea were all-sufficient for human
needs. In the growth and development of
man, as he became educated in relation to
the forces that surrounded him, he began to
make selections, and introduced the order of
cultivation and care to secure the perfection

of the elements on whose assimilation his comfort and happiness so largely depended. This was the first introduction of *productive labor*, and to-day all direct efforts at production are in the line of cultivation and development of existing forces.

Labor, both mental and physical, is nature's great developing process. It not only forms the avenue through which she reveals herself to man, and opens up to him her exhaustless resources, but, at the same time, *unfolds* his *capacity* to become *all-wise, all-good*. This capacity is the *mark of distinction between him* and the *brute;* bearing the traces of infinite principles in his constitution, they express themselves, first, in desire, incentive or want; that want forms the basis of all motive and inquiry, calls out action, which action becomes the means through which the want is supplied; want furnishes the motive, then, that prompts all industrial effort; therefore, to create a full supply for every need of every human being, with the least exhaustion of elements and wear and tear of agents, constitutes the *function* of *industrial science*, and expresses the true relation man sustains to God in material things.

The natural elements and forces, then, together with labor, as relative opposites and mutual dependents, *constitute* the only *creative agencies* for the production of man's supplies. In the creation of the necessaries of life, man, by his intelligence, understanding the functional relation of the natural elements and things to each other, can bring them together, or organize, according to the law of relative opposites in those relations, and thus secure the highest possible results. The same *principles* that *govern matter* in *inanimate nature apply to man*, for, in his physical constitution he is made up of the same elements, only that his higher nature and intelligence enables him to *recognize* the laws of his being, and to *co-operate* with them understandingly.

Man physically, being an outcome from the natural elements, can neither separate himself from them, nor suspend the absolute and omnipotent laws governing his relation thereto; hence, every individual possesses an inherent claim upon these elements, and an inalienable right to their beneficent uses; a *right* to the *credentials* which he receives from the *hand of God in his own organization*, and they are indisputable. But these elements and forces, which are the only source from which man's needs can be supplied, are not productive, except in the ratio that intelligent effort is combined therewith, causing a reciprocal play of forces that result in, not only, the refining of the elements, themselves, that they may give back higher and still higher productions, but constitute the legitimate means of man's unfoldment and his royal road to Salvation.

The application of the principles involved in relative opposites to *Sexology, parentage, population, ownership, education* and *industry combined*, will revolutionize the world. God, the love of the neighbor, will be universal. No more disputes respecting *man's rights, woman's rights, individual rights* and *collective rights*. All these are settled upon the simple and self-evident principle of universal goodness (Justice), leaving no grounds for disputation. It will secure to the individual the highest expression of the relative action of pure wisdom with unselfish love, harmonizing the instinctive, passional, emotional, with the rational-spiritual; thus, cleansing the heart of all impurities, abolishing all intemperate habits, and lifting up body and mind to a *vigorous* condition of action.

It will secure to each individual, a *mutual*

interest in all institutions—*religious, govern-mental* and *financial;* making them *public property*, instead of the *private capital* of emperors, kings, and all that long train of political functionaries, who feed at the public crib at the expense of the public; and who curse humanity by giving examples of abuses which outrage common sense and sear the public conscience as with a hot iron. It will secure a mutual interest in the natural prime elements of production, limited by beneficent uses; thus abrogating all abuse through selfish spoliation, speculative monopolies, nefarious trade and money power.

It will secure a mutual interest in a universal system of integral education and industry combined, through which, only, the natural elements and forces can become the beneficent instruments of universal good to man. Through which the laws governing the spiritual and material universe in their beneficent application shall be discovered, which will secure the only possible deliverance from the tyranny of material and mental slavery; the despotism of political tricksters and arbitrary, unnatural codes of man-made laws.

CHAPTER VI.

Mental and Spiritual Dynamics.
Bridging Over Old Conditions Into the New.
Pathological.

Right thinking does the work,
Immortal youth it brings,—
Death and its shadow throws away;
And life, *eternal* life, in things
Is *seen*, is *felt, tasted* and *touched*—
Becomes the *evidence* to *sense;*
So sense, in turn, is *servant* here below,
Preserver of the *life* in *lower things.*

THE virtue of one culminating period seems to be a relative vice to another culminating period. These periods are self-evident marks of progress in the career and procedure of men and things. It is in order to have, first, the blade, then the blossom, the promise, then the full fruition; from the lower to the higher, from the simple to the complex, from the known to the unknown. The endless combinations of elements constitute the shell, or objective, within which is the kernel—the spiritual intention and its declaration. Earth's rock-written page attests the same in the Azoic, Paleozoic and

Cenezoic periods. Each wrote its history—
then ascended into higher expressions of
planet-life. Vegetable life, which began in
sea-weed, culminated in the palm, the luscious peach and nut trees. Animal life, com-
mencing in the stemless protozoans, ended
in Man. Through the *seeming extermination*
of the lower is the foundation laid for the
higher, *foreshadowing* the highest Love that
would lay down its life for an enemy, thus
revealing the divine intention, the spiritual
force hidden in God's idea.

There is nothing to condemn. The sin,
sickness and death which are so universally
deplored, are only points of change in our
mental vision. All material forms have their
basis in *mind*. All the errors of life to-day,
arise, not from any disorder in the elements
of being, as such, but in imperfect association—the result of immature thinking, which
leads to immature expressions, for thinking
and being are the two relative halves of the
same thing; since what a man knows or
thinks he knows, is one with the mind so
thinking.

We can draw no line between *past, present
and future*—all merging into an *everlasting
now*. Duration has no beginning nor end-

ing, save in the domain of man's senses—
there they constitute the comparative process
of the mind, and present the differential
points of unfoldment in all the senses can
comprehend. Man is surrounded by giant
forces, which are not in themselves comprehended. He lives in a world of effects, until
spiritual perception introduces him into the
realm of causation. Man is a microcosm in
himself; exists, the reflection of all principles
and their formulas; all forces and their po-
tencies. He possesses choice, self-assertion,
self-reliance; and, these have their *fields of
force*, and are complemented by stern necessity and inexorable laws, which are relative
opposites and mutual dependents.

The laws governing this association were
imposed by Infinite Intelligence, and are
cyphered out in the living organism of man
and in universal nature, which should be a
sufficient guarantee to every soul, that the
order of life in its ultimate is perfect, com-
manding: "Be ye also perfect, even as your
Father in Heaven is perfect." This degree
of perfection will be attained when man-made
laws shall be in unison and *not* at variance
with the self-operating laws made manifest
throughout the realm of men and things.

As the angle of divergence, so is the tendency to poverty, pain, injustice, the carnage of bloody warfare; the necessity of training vast armies and navies to the trade of wholesale slaughter; the perpetuation of the hangman and gallows, penitentiary, prison, mad house, and all those barbarous instruments pertaining thereto.

God's fiat and man's free will are relative opposites; the *points* of *divergence* from *their parallelism* constitute the only *curse* that can ever come—the only *evil* that *ever was*, and the only *torment* that *hath sting;* and these are *intensified* and *widened* by the *extent* of the *association, organization* and *co-operative effort* involved in the *use* or *abuse* of any prime element in the domain of man's relations to God in the universe of things.

Co-operation means joint operation. Combinations are joint operations, combined. Organization is a system of ideas upon which combinations are formed.

A combination according to organization is an institution, to wit: Time was when a combination of functionaries who assumed the care of men's souls was designated a Religious Institution.

The barbarous practice of dogmatic laws,

that comprehended little that was remedial, charitable or just, whose final appeal was to the dungeon and gibbet, was a Legal Institution.

Seeking shelter behind the ramparts of legal enactments, converting the human stomach into an apothecary shop, not to mention other kindred cruelties in physics, constitutes a Medical Institution.

A combination which endows a mere promise to pay with functions of reproduction, and converts *credit* into an active agent of revenue, unassociated with intelligence or labor, is a Financial Institution.

A combination standing between producer and consumer, plundering both at the same time, is a Trading Institution.

The anxious, corosive care, weary toil, the enslavement of the forces of the being in the abuses of labor, is the only apology for a scientific system of co-operative industry and education combined.

Incomplete, imperfect ideas, perfectly or imperfectly applied, are the *fountain source*, the producing cause, and the begetting principle of all forms of evil—of crime and the criminal, of sin and the sinner, of sickness in its countless varieties and infinite degrees of manifestation.

Imperfect *Theological Ideas* have reversed the entire order of being; produced an incompetent god; established an eternal divorcement between Creator and the created, making All-wise God, our Eternal Father, the *author* of a personal devil, a local hell, and a system of rewards and punishments which alone could appeal to the lowest selfish instincts in animal life, not to the rational-spiritual in man; they have instituted cruelty, injustice, slavery, both mental and physical; have subjugated the weak to the strong, the less to the greater, through the barbarous weapons of carnal warfare, (the barn-yard law)—the strongest hoof and longest horns—alike under all forms of government, *Theocratic, Democratic, Republic* and *Empire.*

This immature theological idea was reflected upon the conscious thought of mankind, and, since as "men think, so they act," the untruthful relations involved in the untruthful idea, together with its rights and responsibilities, culminated and became circumstantial, *actual.* The fulfillment of these unnatural and untruthful relations, called for the introduction of sacrifices—the plentiful shedding of blood of beasts, not sparing turtle doves and young pigeons, to pacify this mental monster, this idea of an angry god. Huge temples have been reared and consecrated to these practices, wherein the fiery god was worshipped with all fear and trembling.

This fearful idea of an angry god, this oriental conception of Father and Mother-creator, inevitably resulted in all forms of disease—*mental mania*, in all its degrees of madness. These diseases, of necessity, blossom out in, and through, the corporeal principle, which is but a *manifestation* of *mind*. "I, the Mind," or spiritual principle, organize the body through Sexology, through parentage, and the formative force of the environments conferred by the combination, associations and circumstances which this imperfect idea propagated.

Turn back history's page, and behold the cruel, inhuman and relentless warfare — Crusades and Crusaders, which have been inaugurated and sustained by the force of this idea, for the perpetuation of its life and glory; or, to-day, cast a glance across the Atlantic Ocean — to Italy, Spain, Portugal,

and portions of Ireland—where the people,
under its inspiration, pray the most and re-
ceive the least. These countries are cele-
brated for their magnificent temples of
worship, and the *abounding* of the *multitude* of *both prelates* and *paupers* as relative
opposites and mutual dependents.

This imperfect idea is made manifest in
exchange—the system of onerous usury on
unproductive property, falsely called the
philosophy of finance; in the abuses of trade,
extending the privileges of the purchasing
power to the rich, and denying it to the poor,
from which arises "the smaller the parcel the
higher the price;" the introduction of the
tax-gatherer for the sustenance of this empty
carcass, without blood or brains, is a practical
fraud imposed upon intelligence and productive industry; in clothing the lawyer with the
unnatural practice of *law-making* and *law-
enforcing*, instead of *law-discovery*, the spirit
of which is manifest in punishing the *body* for
the *errors* of the *mind, consequent* upon the
imposition of the imperfect idea itself. It is
the begetter of all for which armies, navies
and bludgeoned police are instituted, the
cause of poverty and pauperism, and all disease and vices flowing therefrom.

This idea, like a midnight assassin, has dared to enter into the sacred precincts of Sexology, confining the marital right and responsibility to a public acknowledgement of the same before a functionary of the church or state, instead of educating and enforcing, by obedience, the sacred science it involves; which would result in the begetting of a healthy and efficient population, and in the entire prevention of adultery, divorce, and ten thousand other imbecilities, all the legitimate offspring of this imperfect idea, "perfectly or imperfectly applied."

This oriental trinity in unity, this child of polygamous origin, to wit:

First: An ideal, personal, vindictive god, the fury of whose justice could be satisfied only by the shedding of blood through the plentiful sacrifice of animal life.

Second: An ideal, personal devil and imps, specially endowed by this ideal, wrathful god with attributes to lure astray the innocent and unwary.

Third: An ideal, local hell, presided over by Beelzebub, who administers its torments, its *living death*, everlasting burning yet never consumed, with no possible escape, no remote redemption, (with a furious inspiration too horrible to contemplate or describe,) has flooded the rivers of life, opened wide the gates of false habit and custom, making veritable the saying: "Man is born unto trouble as the sparks fly upward."

Wonderful! that such a preposterous idea could have been entertained for one moment and made the formative force in mental dynamics; yet, its psychological influence has been such that it has been proclaimed from the pulpit by specially qualified doctors of divinity, been sanctioned by the public press, has constituted largely the literature of the ages, was the inspiration of the poet, taught in the schools, seminaries, colleges and universities.

It has—*this delusive idea*—*has threaded* its devious way into the warp and woof of the entire social fabric, expressing itself in the barbarous manners and customs of the centuries.

This was the seed! *What* the harvest? Fearful! Full of fear! Fear of God! Fear of devils; fear of hell-fire; fear of death! Fear of the *curse* upon *maternity;* fear of *poverty* through the *curse* upon the earth; fear of the *curse* upon *labor;* hence penal servitude—Slavery!

The revenge of this imaginary god was *infectious—contagious.* It became the model after whose pattern every judgment was formulated, this arbitrary curse forming its precedent. Revenge and Fear are *relative opposites;* and, in their individual or collective expressions are the sources of all diseases in their positive and negative types. Revenge, Envy, Jealousy, and their kindred qualities, blossom out in the body in the form of the *positive series*, or *groups*, of so-called disease—from *fevers*, scarlet as hell-fire, gradually down to the low *intermitting fret*, which noiselessly devours the vital forces; while on the other side, the reacting force of *fear* in *doubt, becomes* the *parent* of the *negative series*, whose name is *Legion*.

The modern religious *revivalist* little dreams of what *he* does under the excitement of this idea; how he psychologizes his audience, and by his allusions and vigorous appeals to what is involved in this oriental scheme, inoculates the unborn child, through the listening mother, with the virus of Fear which must inevitably produce the so-called *run* of *diseases in children.*

The unnatural action of this idea can be explained on no other hypothesis than that

"A lie in Heaven is truth in Hell," and *vice
versa*. Beneficent use in natural relations
represents the *heavenly condition;* the misuse
or abuse of true relations, or the substitution
of false or erroneous ones therefor, represents the latter conditions.

Absolutely there can be no possible sickness or sin; the good God never made any.
In the beneficent uses of things, which ex-
tends through the senses, functions and organs of the body, all is harmonious, all divine.
But misuse, through ignorance or otherwise,
of the good, is terminally converted into evil,
harmony into discord, truth into error, health
into sickness, pleasure into pain.   This law is
fortuitous.   It drives mankind back out of
misuse and abuse, torment being the index
to the false condition.   Sin and sickness are
self-corrective, circumstantial, being the out-
flow of the abuse of use.

The investigation of the causes of sin,
which is the true diagnosis of disease, is not
pleasurable to the sensuous life.   But "My
Physician, Mind," would deeply probe, would
thrust the lancet of intelligent investigation
to the *center* and *core* of the *polluted* ulcer, a
false civilization, which enslaves the masses
of mankind and prostitutes the finer forces

to degraded uses.   These conditions *must be uncovered.*   Ere the stream can cease to flow the fountain must be dried.   Ere its cancerous, devouring fire can be quenched, its producing roots must be extracted, and its psychological chain of bondage must be broken.

CHAPTER VII.

The cure, the cure, is *quick*, is *sure*,
Sin and sickness cannot endure;
But vanish like the morning dew
When the full sunlight comes in view.
The light of Truth doth soon dispel
The *fear* of Sin — the fear of Hell —
Sin and disease will flee away
Before the Truth's illumining ray.

THEORY precedes Practice. As is the idea, so is the result—the former is causative, the latter formative. First the plan, then the structure. If the premises be true, the conclusions may be also; for, the universal rule is (all things being equal) "Like begets like."

Truth is the strong man, "Kwasind," here below, even in the domain of the personal senses. To truly know the truth of Truth, is to be *one with Truth.* An *intellectual* appreciation of truth merely reaches the *shell* —does not touch the kernel. To love the truth is to absorb its inmost soul, and to express its potency through active and passive

[61]

endeavor. Love, Life, Truth, are trinity in
unity, and unity in trinity. Man is the
quality, the fountain-source of Life, Truth
and Love; these are the primal elements of
his being, and underlie his very constitution,
from which he cannot alienate himself or be
alienated by any external circumstance or
condition.

Everything relative has a career, a process
of development or self-assertion; this career
and self-affirmation is in connection with some
other career, some other process of self-
assertion, whose rights and responsibilities
are of the same nature and kind. These
forces are correlative, co-operative, mutual;
they are each individual, particular and separate; yet, they are the outcome of a vast and
stupendous unity—oneness—wholeness.

These two elements of being constitute
the sovereignty of the individuality, and the
sovereignty of every other individuality; and
these individualities being alike, and at the
same time unlike, form the basement of
thought upon which the superstructure of
mind must be reared. A thought embracing
but one premise is like unto a bird with one
wing, or as scissors with one blade; as such
is, in the order of things, *out* of *order*.

In the career of the universe and man there are marked epochs—culminating periods—in which transition and transfiguration take place. These careers are not to be confounded or lost sight of, but are to be noticed at the same time as the unit of life is noticed, for they are the links in the universal chain of being, and must be so cognized. Between the culminating periods of existence there are processes of unfoldment, with beginnings, intermediates and terminations, which again repeat themselves in other following processes, and on, and on, without beginning, end, or change, when viewed in the unbroken cycle of the soul's existence.

The correct view, then, is the association of the finite, or relative, with the infinite, or absolute; to *dis-associate* these in the mind, is to become sick. To unlink the mortal and immortal, to separate the love and emotion from the wisdom and intelligent principle, is mental mania—things only half-born, cakes only half-cooked. The mere intellectual denial of matter does not wipe matter out of existence; but such a denial may, for the time, blind the eye to its reality. To affirm that sin and sickness are the beliefs of the

personal senses, does not change the inexorable order manifested in God's idea; but it
may draw a vail over the senses, and tem-
porarily hide the miscreant of false use in
abuse from outer consciousness.

To affirm that intellectual prate, either in
denying or affirming, can permanently heal
the sick, is an error, and the sooner it is
abandoned the sooner the deception will dis-
appear. A positive affirmation or a positive
denial, is not in the letter, and cannot be em-
braced in a mental argument; it is a *spiritual
force*, not as yet capable of definition by the
intellect, for it lies *above* and *beyond* its limitations.

A *positive denial* of the existence of a
thought or thing is the *annihilation* of the
thought or thing. To affirm a thought or
thing, is the creation of the thought or thing,
provided, *always*, that the denial or affirmation is in harmony with God's idea, or the
order instituted in universal nature; otherwise, it only lingers as a psychological
shadow for a little while in the domain of
the mind so denying or so affirming.

The inexorable law of being is such that
the less must conform to the greater, but not
to *lose itself in that conformation*, or to be ab-

sorbed thereby. Individuality is individuality, *indestructible, immortal, eternal.* The types of life are relative, yet each type is individualized. Typical illustrations are found in the tree, the animal, Man. All are *living beings,* but their typical illustrations consist in the limitations of their functional use.

The earth is man's footstool—ordinated by Infinite Intelligence—with ample means, provisions and facilities to fulfill the divine intention in its creation. The earth is man's inheritance, man's birthright; indeed, man's physical is antetyped by the earth and its relations.

The earth has its atmosphere, its circulatory system within itself, and again repeated in its relations to other bodies—the sun and sister orbs. The inferior extremities and viscera correspond to the earth—the respiratory organs, to the atmosphere—the head, to the celestial sphere. The viscera has its caloric center in the stomach and its connected glands. These elements, again, are connected with and upheld by the oxygen and other atmospheric elements, received through the lungs.

The Spirit—the Law-giver—under whose action the electrical and magnetic forces are compelled to polarize every molecule that enters into the entire structure of the human body, performs its function through the head, the center of the nervous system. The polarity of the human physical structure, also that of the earth and its atmosphere, are alike subject to mental and spiritual dynamics.

"My Physician, Mind," asserts the supremacy of this principle, not only as a universal panacea in the removal of all moral and physical ailments, but constitutes a perfect prevention to all disease, whether in acute or chronic form.

TOPEKA,

Headquarters in the State of Kansas,

FOR

"My Physician, Mind."

A CENTER

For the Culture and Practical Application of the Divine Principle of Cure.

Classes for Instruction formed Monthly.

Patients can be treated at the Center, in their homes or absently.

Correspondence invited.

153 Madison St., Topeka, Kansas.

E. S. ROBINSON, M. S., Principal.

MISSOURI

Metaphysical University,

AND HYGIENIC INSTITUTE.

Full Course of Instruction in the Divine Science of Life,

All diseases both of body and mind eternally set aside—cast into oblivion!—by a purely mental process.

Ironton is located directly on the I. M. & S. R. R., eighty-eight miles from the city of St. Louis, in the beautiful valley of the Arcadia. It is the highest land between the Gulf of Mexico and the city of Quincy, Ill. Climate, tonic; scenery, mountainous.

Pupils and invalids will find this Institute replete with home comforts and a restful element.

TERMS LIBERAL. CORRESPONDENCE SOLICITED,

J. B. CROCKER, Proprietor.